Amelia Jane
Again

By Enid Blyton

Naughty Amelia Jane
Amelia Jane Is Naughty Again
Amelia Jane Gets Into Trouble
Amelia Jane Again
Good Idea, Amelia Jane

The Adventures of the Wishing-Chair
The Wishing-Chair Again
More Wishing-Chair Stories
The Wishing-Chair Collection

The Enchanted Wood
The Magic Faraway Tree
The Folk of the Faraway Tree
Up the Faraway Tree
The Magic Faraway Tree Collection

The Caravan Family
The Seaside Family
The Buttercup Farm Family
The Queen Elizabeth Family
Are We There Yet?

Amelia Jane
Again

Enid Blyton

EGMONT

EGMONT

We bring stories to life

First published in Great Britain 1946 by Newnes
This edition published in 2019 by Egmont UK Limited
The Yellow Building, 1 Nicholas Road, London W11 4AN

Enid Blyton ®, The Magic Faraway Tree ®
and Enid Blyton's signature are registered trade marks of
Hodder & Stoughton Limited
Text © 1946 Hodder & Stoughton Limited
Illustrations © 2019 Hodder & Stoughton Limited
Illustrated by Erin Brown

ISBN 978 1 4052 9324 2

www.egmont.co.uk

A CIP catalogue record for this title is available from the British Library

Printed and bound by the CPI Group

33140/001

Contents

Amelia Jane and the Shoes

Now once the toys in the nursery had a party and they didn't ask that big naughty doll, Amelia Jane. She didn't even know they were going to have a party until she saw them setting the table, and smelt the cakes cooking on the little stove in the dolls' house.

'Oooh!' said Amelia Jane, pleased. 'A party! This *is* a surprise!'

The teddy bear looked at her. 'It will be an even greater surprise to you when you find you're not coming!' he said. 'We're a bit tired of you and your tricks. A party will be very nice without you!'

'Eeee-eee-eee!' laughed the clockwork

mouse, and the other toys giggled too. Amelia Jane went red.

'You nasty, horrid things!' she said. 'Well, have your party then! I'm sure I don't want to come. I've better things to do than come to silly little parties like yours!'

She went off into the corner in a huff. The toys giggled again. Amelia Jane was funny when she was in a huff. She pouted her mouth and wrinkled her nose and tossed her thick yellow hair.

The party began. It was a lovely one, with tiny chocolate cakes to eat, small pink sweets out of the toy sweetshop, and lemonade to drink. The toys played blindman's-buff, and musical chairs, and general post, so they really did have a fine time. Amelia Jane pretended to be reading a book,

but all the time she was really peeping at the party, and making up her naughty little mind that she would think of some trick to punish the little toys.

Now after a bit the toys wanted to dance. It was quieter to dance with their shoes off, so they all sat down, took off their shoes, and piled them in a heap near the dolls' house. Then they set the musical-box going, and began to dance with one another.

Amelia Jane saw the shoes in a big pile. She grinned to herself. What would the toys say if those suddenly disappeared? That would be funny!

So, when the toys were all busy dancing in and out and round about, Amelia Jane crept up to the shoes, stuffed them into the apron of her dress, and ran off again. Nobody noticed her.

Amelia Jane sat in a dark corner of the nursery with the shoes, wondering where to hide them. Nearby was a mouse-hole.

Oooh! thought Amelia. If I stuff these shoes down the mouse-hole, no one will find them. What fun!

So she stuffed the little shoes down the mouse-hole. There were leather shoes and woollen socks, kid shoes and felt shoes, some with laces, some with buttons, some with nothing at all. They all went down that mousehole.

Well, when the dancing was over the toys ran to put their shoes on again. But they weren't there! They stared all around, very puzzled.

'I'm sure we put them here,' said the clockwork clown.

'Well, where are they?' asked the curly-haired doll. 'Shoes can't walk!'

'That's just what they can do!' said the clockwork mouse smartly.

'Not unless there are feet in them,' said the teddy bear, rather crossly. He wore woollen socks, and they kept his feet warm at night. He did hope they weren't lost.

'I'm sure Amelia Jane knows something about our shoes,' said the clockwork clown suddenly. The toys went over to her.

'Amelia Jane, what have you done with our shoes?' asked the teddy bear.

Amelia Jane looked so surprised that her eyebrows shot up into her hair. '*Shoes*!'

she said. 'Shoes! Whatever do you mean?'

'Oh come, Amelia, you know quite well what shoes are!' said the clown crossly. 'What – have – you – done – with – our – SHOES?'

'Well, really!' said Amelia Jane. 'Why should you think I've done anything with them? Do you suppose I came and took them off your feet?'

'No, we don't suppose anything so silly,' said the bear. 'But we do feel perfectly sure you've taken the pile of shoes and hidden them somewhere.'

'Well, you can go on supposing,' said Amelia Jane rudely, and she began to read her book again. Not another word would she say.

The toys hated going without their shoes. Their feet were cold, and the teddy bear trod on a pin and yelled so loudly that the jack-in-the-box sprang out to see what the matter was. Not until the next night did Amelia Jane say what she had done.

All the toys were round her, begging for

their shoes, and Amelia Jane looked at them, her cheeky face red with delight. 'Yes, I *did* take your shoes!' she said. 'I thought I would punish you for not asking me to your party.'

'Well, where did you *put* them?' asked the bear impatiently. 'Hurry up and tell us.'

'I pushed them down the mouse-hole,' said Amelia Jane, grinning.

'Pushed them down the *mouse*-hole!' cried all the toys, in astonishment. 'Oh, you naughty doll! Get them at once.'

'Get them yourself,' said Amelia Jane. '*I'm* not going to bother!'

So the clockwork mouse was sent into the mouse-hole to fetch out everybody's shoes. But, oh dear, oh dear, when he came back with them one by one, what an upset there was!

The little brown mice down the hole had bitten and chewed the shoes, meaning to make their new nest of them – and they were full of holes now.

'How dreadful!' groaned the clown. 'They're quite spoilt. Oh, you are a very naughty girl, Amelia Jane! Look at our shoes!'

Amelia was really sorry to see what had

happened, but she wouldn't say so.

The toys put on their shoes, and went back to the toy-cupboard, very upset.

The next day, when the children saw the nibbled shoes, they were most surprised. 'Look!' they said. 'The mice have been eating our toys' shoes. What a shame! We will take some money out of our money-box and buy them some more, and we'll knit the bear some nice new socks.'

So it wasn't very long before all the toys had fine new shoes and socks, better than their old ones, and they were very pleased indeed! But Amelia Jane wasn't pleased! She felt cross. She hadn't got any new shoes. It was too bad.

So what do you think she did? She took off her nice blue shoes, which were made of warm felt, and went to push them down the mouse-hole! But they were too big to go down, so Amelia Jane took them to the window, and threw them out! Perhaps they wouldn't be found – and then she too would have some new ones!

But, dear me, the two children were very cross with Amelia Jane when they found that her shoes were missing. 'You have lost them!' they said. 'You are getting very careless with your clothes, Amelia Jane. What you want is a good scolding.'

And they gave her such a scolding that she cried a puddle on to the floor. *What* a shock for naughty Amelia Jane!

But that wasn't the end of it. No – the children found her shoes out in the garden, where she had thrown them, wet through

with the rain. They dried them and put them on Amelia's feet again. But they had shrunk smaller with the rain, and they were dreadfully tight. Really, poor Amelia could hardly walk!

'I'm sorry I played about with your shoes,'

Amelia Jane wept to the toys. 'I've been punished – and you've all got nice new shoes – and *my* shoes are old and tight and hurt me! I'm very miserable.'

So the kind-hearted toys took off her shoes, and stretched them by pulling hard. Then they fitted Amelia Jane properly, and she dried her eyes and was very grateful.

'I won't play tricks again,' she said. 'I really won't.'

But nobody believed her – and I'm afraid I don't either!

It Serves You Right, Amelia Jane

Once, when the children were away, there came such a fine sunny day that the toys longed to go out in the daytime, instead of waiting till night.

'I don't see why we shouldn't,' said the bear. 'There's no one about. Let's go and have a picnic in the orchard at the bottom of the garden.'

'Oh yes,' said Amelia Jane at once.

'Not *you*,' said the clown. 'You don't behave yourself well enough. You can stay here. You're not asked to the picnic.'

'Well, I shall come all the same,' said

Amelia, annoyed. 'So there!'

And she did. The toys couldn't stop her, for she was such a big, strong doll. She tossed her yellow hair in the air, smoothed down her red frock, and said 'Pooh!' whenever any toy said she was not to come.

'It's too bad!' said Tom the toy soldier, as he carried a basket of goodies down to the orchard. 'Amelia Jane has such a big appetite that she will eat far more than her share, and she's such a nuisance, always upsetting everyone and teasing them.'

'I wish we could put her somewhere that she couldn't get away from,' said the clockwork mouse. 'She's taken my key away once already today, and you know I won't be able to go all the way down to the orchard unless I'm wound up at least twice.'

'It's a pity she couldn't climb a tree and not be able to get down!' said the bear.

'I've got some butterscotch for us to eat, and once Amelia sees it she will eat the lot!'

'I might be able to make her climb a tree,' said Tom suddenly, with a little giggle.

'Look, here's a fine place for a picnic, just under this old apple tree. Now, you watch me, and see if I don't get Amelia out of our way!'

The toys put down the baskets and packets they were carrying, and watched. Tom ran up to the tree and pretended to try to climb it. But he kept slipping back, and of course Amelia Jane laughed and laughed at him.

'Well, Amelia,' said Tom at last, 'you may laugh all you like, but *you* couldn't climb this tree either! It is very difficult. I did so want to get up it, because I hear you can see for miles around if you are at the top. But not even *you* could climb it!'

'Pooh!' said Amelia Jane at once. She was full of 'poohs' that day. 'I could easily climb it.'

'You couldn't,' said Tom.

'I could,' said Amelia.

'You couldn't!' cried everyone in glee, seeing the trick that the toy soldier was playing.

'Well, I'll just show you, then!' cried Amelia, and she ran to the tree. But it really was rather difficult, because there was a big length of bare trunk before the branches began. Tom pushed Amelia up. All the toys came round and helped.

Whoosh! Amelia Jane shot up the trunk and came to where she could hold on to the branches. She was pleased that the toys were being so kind.

'Thank you!' she said. 'You are very helpful, Toys.'

'Don't mention it!' said Tom politely. 'We are pleased to push you up a tree.'

Amelia Jane began to climb up and up, feeling very proud. Ha, she could do what the other toys couldn't! She was a fine strong doll, and she would soon be at the top of the tree, and looking for miles around the country.

The toys took no more notice of her. They quickly undid their baskets and packets, sat down and began to enjoy their picnic in the green shade of the old apple tree. The sun lay in freckles of gold on the ground, and the clockwork mouse sat first on one freckle and then on another. It was fun.

'Hi, Toys, you're not watching me!' came Amelia Jane's voice suddenly from the top of the tree. 'Where are you? Look! I'm at the top of the tree! I can see such a lot of things.'

Nobody answered her. The toys grinned at

one another, and Tom handed round some chocolate buns. The bear undid his packet of butterscotch. Everyone was very happy because naughty Amelia Jane wasn't there.

Amelia grew angry. She began to climb down the tree. She came to the lowest branches and peeped between the leaves. She saw the toys picnicking happily, and she was very angry.

'Toys! You've started without me! Oh, you mean things! I'm coming down at once!'

But she couldn't get down from the branches to the ground, for the jump was too big for her.

'Come and help me, Tom!' she shouted. 'You pushed me up – now you can help me down.'

The toy soldier didn't move. He took a bit

22

of butterscotch and chewed it. It was lovely.

Amelia Jane was red with rage.

'I shall miss the picnic!' she cried. 'I shall miss the picnic.'

'You can't miss what you haven't been asked to,' said Tom, giggling.

'Eeee, eeee, eeee!' laughed the clockwork mouse.

'I want some butterscotch too!' squealed Amelia Jane.

'Well, go on wanting,' said the clown.

'Eeee, eeee, eeee!' laughed the mouse again. He thought it was all very funny.

'Oh, you mean things, you got me up this tree just to put me out of the way!' wept Amelia.

'Amelia Jane, you wanted to show how wonderful you were at climbing trees,' said Tom. 'Well, you've done what you wanted. And we've done what we wanted too! We've had a picnic without you. And now we are going to play games. Come on, Toys, let's play cowboys.'

So they did, and hide-and-seek too, and ball. Amelia Jane had to sit up on the branch of the apple tree and watch, and she didn't like it at all. She sulked and she cried.

'Cowboys is a silly game!' she shouted rudely.

'Well, we're not asking *you* to play it!' said the clown.

'Eeee, eeee, eeee!' giggled the mouse.

'If that clockwork mouse giggles any more, I'll smack him!' said Amelia, weeping tears of rage.

'Come and smack me, then!' squealed the mouse, and he ran off, laughing.

Not until the toys were ready to go home again did they help Amelia Jane down. She was hungry and cross, and she felt rather ashamed of herself.

'Look, Amelia, we saved you a bun,' said the teddy bear, holding one out to her. 'We are sorry you were upset, but you shouldn't make yourself such a nuisance!'

'Thank you for the bun,' said Amelia in a small voice, and she ate it, though it was rather squashed, because the bear had sat on it by mistake.

'We'll ask you to our picnic next time, Amelia, if you'll be good,' said the toys.

'Well, I *will* be good then,' said Amelia Jane. But I really don't think she can be!

Amelia Jane Gets a Fright

Once Amelia Jane, the big naughty doll,
thought it would be very funny to give
everyone in the nursery a fright.

So she hid under the table behind the
cushion, and when the sailor doll walked that
way, she growled like a dog and pounced out
at him.

It was dark under the table and the sailor
doll really did think that there was a dog
there. He screamed and fled away to the
toy-cupboard.

'What's the matter? What's the matter?'
cried all the toys.

'There's a very fierce dog under the table,'

said the sailor doll, shaking like a jelly. 'Or it might be a dragon. It was fierce enough.'

Amelia Jane nearly burst with trying not to laugh. She crouched down and hoped somebody else would come. Soon Tom the toy soldier came tiptoeing under the table, keeping a good look out for any fierce dog or dragon. Amelia Jane gave a deep growl.

Tom looked scared. He stopped.

'Urrrrr–grrrrr–urrrr!' said Amelia Jane, and she scrabbled at the floor as if she had claws.

'It's a dragon!' shouted Tom, and fled away so fast that he fell over the rug and went down on his nose. Amelia Jane let out a screech of laughter. The toys thought it was the howl of a dragon and they shivered in the cupboard.

Nobody would go under the table any more that night, and Amelia Jane grew tired of hiding there. She thought she would play another trick on the toys, so she crept quietly out from under the table, climbed on to a chair, and took an apple from the dish of fruit there.

She sat on the table and scraped out two eyes in the apple and a big mouth.

She stuck a hazelnut hard into the apple for a nose. How funny it looked!

Amelia Jane laughed to herself, and crept down from the table with the apple-face. She found a pen with a sharp nib in the children's pencil-box and stuck the apple-face on to it. Then she crept round to the side of the toy-cupboard, where all the toys were sitting, listening for any sign of the dragon under the table.

Amelia Jane made a little squeaky noise. 'Eeeeee! Eeeeee! Eeeeeee!'

Everyone looked up. 'What was that?' said the teddy bear.

'It sounded like the clockwork mouse,' said the golden-haired doll.

'It wasn't, though,' said the clockwork mouse from his corner behind the brick-box.

'I'm here, and I didn't make a sound.'

'Eeee! Eeeee!' said Amelia Jane again, getting her apple-face on its pen-holder, so that she might stick it round the toy-cupboard door as soon as any toy peeped out.

'It's funny,' said the sailor doll. 'That's not a dragon. It sounded like a mouse or a bird or something.'

'I'll peep out and see,' said the teddy bear boldly. So he put his snout outside the cupboard door and tried to see what was squeaking.

And naughty Amelia Jane at once pushed her funny apple-face at the bear! How scared he was! He rushed back into the farthest corner of the toy-cupboard and squeezed down by the clockwork mouse.

'What was it?' cried all the toys.

'It was a face,' said the bear, trembling.

'A *face*!' said Tom scornfully. 'Well, what sort of a body had the face got?'

'It hadn't got a body,' said the bear. 'But it can't be a face,' said the sailor doll. 'I shall look.'

So he looked – and Amelia Jane pushed her

apple-face round the door and made it jig up and down, so that not only the sailor doll could see it but everybody else could too!

'Go away!' cried Tom to the apple-face. The apple-face grinned widely, and jigged up and down again peeping round the door. But Amelia Jane knocked it by mistake against the door and the hazelnut nose fell off!

The sailor doll picked up the nose and found that it was only a nut! He looked at the face and shouted: 'It's just a silly apple-face, that's all! Don't be scared, Toys – it's just a silly apple-face!'

The toys rushed at the face and pulled it off the penholder. They saw Amelia Jane peeping round the corner, laughing till the tears ran down her cheeks, and they were very angry. Tom threw the apple-face at her, but Amelia dodged, and the apple knocked over a castle that the children had built of bricks. It fell with a crash.

'Sh! Sh!' said the bear. 'You'll wake the whole house up! Amelia Jane, how dare you frighten us all like that? Wasting a good apple too! I suppose you were the fierce dog or dragon under the table as well?'

'Yes,' said Amelia Jane, laughing all over her big face. 'Oh, it's such fun to frighten you, Toys. You are such a lot of sillies! Fancy being scared of an apple-face! I shall go on thinking of tricks to frighten you. It makes me laugh!'

The toys got in the toy-cupboard and shut the door. They were very angry with Amelia. They whispered about her, and tried to think how to stop her.

'If only we knew where she was every minute, we'd know it was Amelia and not dragons and things,' said Tom.

The clockwork mouse spoke up.

'Well, let's do something so that we always *do* know where Amelia Jane is!' he said. 'There are some bells in the bead-box that came off the old reins. Couldn't the golden-haired doll sew them on to the under-hem of Amelia's skirt when she is asleep? Then wherever she went we should hear a little tinkling and know where she was!'

'Good idea!' said everyone, and they laughed. It was funny to think of Amelia Jane tinkling as she walked. They opened the door and peeped round it. Amelia Jane was sound asleep, tired out with all her tricks. Very quietly the golden-haired doll took the tiny

bells from the bead-box and went up to Amelia Jane.

It didn't take a minute to sew two little bells on to the under-hem of her skirt. The golden-haired doll giggled and ran back to the cupboard.

And now it was no use Amelia Jane hiding anywhere to jump out at the toys, because they always heard the little tinkle that told them where she was! So Amelia didn't manage to give anyone a scare at all for the next few nights, and she was cross.

She couldn't *think* where the tinkle came from – but at last she found the little bells. She *was* angry! She pulled them off her skirt, and then she pinned them to the curtain by the window. Every time the wind blew the curtain the bells tinkled!

37

'Amelia Jane is behind the curtain!' whispered the toys to one another. But she wasn't! It was only the bells tinkling there. Amelia was hiding in the cupboard, meaning to jump at the toys when they came in. And what a fright she gave them!

'She's taken off her bells!' cried Tom. 'We must think of something else!'

They hustled Amelia Jane out of their cupboard and slammed the door. Amelia laughed and climbed into the dolls' cot. The dolls were not there. They were in the toy-cupboard, talking.

'Well, they won't be able to sleep *here* tonight!' said Amelia, and she snuggled down comfortably and went to sleep.

'You know,' said Tom to the toys in the cupboard, 'there's only one thing to do to stop Amelia Jane from scaring us. And that's to scare *her*!'

'Let's!' shouted the toys.

'But how?' asked the bear.

'There are a lot of brown stockings in the dolls' trunk,' said Tom, grinning. 'What about getting them out, sewing them neatly together, and pretending they are a long snake?'

'But how will that frighten Amelia Jane?' asked the sailor doll.

'Well, we'll pin the stocking-snake on to the back of her shoe,' grinned Tom. 'Then we'll say there's a snake after her – and no matter how she runs away from it, it will follow her because it will be fastened to her! Don't you remember how she once put a plasticine tail on to the bear?'

'Oh, good!' said the toys. They ran to get the brown stockings. The golden-haired doll sewed them neatly together till they looked like a wriggly brown snake. Then she tiptoed to the cot where Amelia Jane lay asleep. She pinned the stocking-snake to the back of Amelia's shoe.

'Now we must all make a noise and shout out that there is a snake loose in the nursery!' said Tom. 'We must pretend we are very frightened.'

So they began to shout and make a noise. 'Ooh, a snake! Look out, a snake! A snake!'

Amelia Jane woke and sat up. She was afraid of snakes.

'Where is it?' she cried.

'We think it went into your cot!' shouted the toys. 'Look! There it is in your cot,

Amelia! Run!'

Amelia screamed and jumped from the cot, but as the stocking-snake was pinned to the back of her shoe, it had to come after her wherever she went! Oh dear! how Amelia screamed and ran and dodged! It wasn't a bit of use, the snake went wherever she did!

'It's biting my foot, it's biting my foot!' she squealed. 'Save me, Toys, save me!'

But the toys were laughing too much to do anything. Amelia ran and ran. 'Go away, you horrid snake! Go after the others! Oh, Toys, save me, and I promise never to scare you again!'

'Do you mean that promise?' asked the teddy bear at once. 'Very well – I will save you from the snake – though it would have served you right if it had eaten you up.'

He ran to Amelia and undid the pin. Then he waved the stocking-snake in her face.

'You made an apple-face – and we made a stocking-snake!' he said. 'Ho, ho, Amelia Jane, it *was* fun to see you running away from a row of brown stockings!'

Amelia was angry. She stalked off to the

dolls' cot again and didn't say another word. But the toys said plenty – and how they did laugh! Amelia wouldn't scare them again in a hurry!

Amelia Jane in the Country

Now you remember that the toys told Amelia Jane she could come with them to their next picnic if she was good, don't you? Well, the big doll managed to be fairly good for a few days – and then the teddy bear thought it would be fine to go for a day in the country.

'Can I come too?' asked Amelia Jane.

'You haven't been *very* good,' said the bear, rather sternly.

'Well, I haven't been very bad either,' said Amelia. 'I've only put salt in your tea once, instead of sugar – and I've not taken away the mouse's key at all.'

'Yes, but you have kicked a marble up into

the air and made it fall into my jug of milk at teatime,' said Tom the toy soldier.

'I couldn't help that,' said Amelia. 'I didn't know you were going to put your milk on the table just then.'

'Well, don't let's quarrel,' said the clown. 'She can come if she doesn't do anything silly. How shall we go? It's a long way to the country.'

'The wooden train will take some of us, and the bus too, and the motor-car can take two or three,' said Tom. So it was all arranged. The golden-haired doll did some cooking on the stove, and made buns and biscuits. Tom took an apple from the fruit-dish. If he cut it up into slices there would be plenty for everyone.

They got into the train, the car, and the

bus. There was just room for everyone,
though Amelia Jane had to ride on the boiler
of the engine because she was so big! She
didn't mind that – she thought it was fun.

'I'm going to take my butterfly-net with me,' she said, just before they started. 'I might be able to catch some butterflies.'

'No, don't do that,' said Tom. 'It isn't kind to catch the pretty things. Leave your net behind.'

But Amelia Jane wouldn't. She stuck it down the funnel of the engine and off they went, the butterfly-net looking most peculiar waggling about in the funnel!

It was lovely out in the country. The sun shone, the daisies smiled everywhere, and the bees hummed like tiny aeroplanes. Amelia Jane was so happy that she went quite mad! She ran all over the place, shouting and laughing. She took her butterfly-net and began to try to catch the big white butterflies that flew everywhere.

But the butterflies wouldn't be caught! Not one of those white ones could Amelia catch. So she hunted the little blue ones – but they were very nimble and soared high into the air long before Amelia could get her net down on them.

'Amelia Jane, do stop rushing about trying to catch butterflies that won't be caught,' said Tom. 'You make me feel quite hot, watching you tear about.'

'Well, don't watch then,' said Amelia, racing after a red-and-black butterfly.

'Look, Amelia, that's a Red Admiral!' said the bear, proud of knowing the butterfly's name. But Amelia didn't know he was talking about a butterfly. She thought he meant a red sailor – a real admiral! She looked all around for him.

'And there goes a Painted Lady!' cried the bear proudly, as a pretty, gaily coloured butterfly fluttered past. 'Oh, and there's a Peacock! You can't catch those, Amelia Jane!'

'Of course I can't catch a red sailor or a lady or a peacock bird!' cried Amelia Jane. 'Don't be silly! But where's the famous sailor, Teddy Bear? I can't see an admiral anywhere. And where's the lady, all painted up? I can't see her either. And I'm sure there isn't a lovely peacock about, showing off its beautiful tail!'

The toys squealed with laughter. 'She thinks they are real people and birds!' giggled the sailor doll. 'She doesn't know they are only names of pretty butterflies. Silly Amelia Jane!'

Well, if there was one thing that Amelia

hated, it was being called silly. She lost her temper and rushed at the toys.

'I can't catch admirals and ladies and peacocks,' she said, 'but I'll catch a sailor and a doll and a mouse. So there!'

She brought her butterfly-net down over the surprised sailor doll, and there he was, caught! Amelia Jane laughed with delight. She twisted the net over, and there was the sailor doll bobbing about, terribly afraid of falling out.

Amelia tipped him out, bump!

What a bruise he got! Then the naughty doll ran to catch the golden-haired doll, who swallowed a crumb down the wrong way in alarm and began to choke. Amelia caught her up neatly in her net. She swung her up in the air and tipped her out, bump!

'I'm catching butterflies, I'm catching butterflies!' sang Amelia Jane joyfully. She ran after the clockwork mouse, who scuttled away at once. But his clockwork soon ran down and Amelia caught him up. Up he went in the net – and down he came, bump! His key was knocked out and flew off into the grass. The sailor at once went to hunt for it, because if it was lost the mouse would never be able to run again.

'Amelia Jane, stop!' shouted all the toys

in a rage. 'Stop!'

'I'm catching butterflies, I'm catching butterflies!' sang Amelia, and she caught all the toys with her long net, one after another, tipping them out, bump, as soon as she had swung them up into the air! Oh, she was behaving very badly indeed!

'We'll never, never trust you again, Amelia Jane,' said the teddy bear angrily. 'We'll never speak to you again. You've spoilt the picnic. You are a tiresome, naughty doll, and we shall leave you behind here. We don't want you ever to come back to the nursery again!'

They climbed into the train, the car, and the bus. They wouldn't let Amelia Jane ride on the engine boiler as she had when they came. They pushed her off. They wouldn't let her ride with them at all.

'But I shall be lost all by myself here,' wept Amelia, really frightened. 'Don't leave me behind.'

'Amelia Jane, this time we mean what we say,' said Tom, starting the engine. 'We don't want you, and we don't care what becomes of you. Goodbye!'

And off they started, chuff-chuff-chuff-r-r-r-r-r, rumble-umble-umble! Amelia Jane watched them go, and she wept bitterly, for she knew that she could never find her way back to the nursery alone.

But, oh dear – a dreadful thing happened! The train somehow took the wrong path. It took the path that led to the river – and do you know, before it could stop itself it had run right into the water – splash!

Into the river went the toys, struggling and

splashing. The little duck could swim, but no one else. They began to shout and splutter. 'Help! Help! Help!'

Now the car and bus had managed to stop in time, and the toys inside them ran to help the others.

But they couldn't reach them. Whatever were they to do? Everyone began to shout and sob and cry.

Amelia Jane heard the noise, for the engine had not gone very far before it fell into the river. The big doll listened in surprise. What was happening? She dried her tears and set off to see. When she turned the corner she stared in astonishment and fright. The golden-haired doll was struggling in the river, and the pink rabbit, and the clockwork mouse! Tom was there too, sinking for the third time.

Now Amelia was naughty but she wasn't bad, and as soon as she saw that dreadful sight she was as upset as the rest of the toys. She rushed to the river at once, shouting, 'Save them, save them!'

'We can't!' wept the toys. 'We can't reach!'

And then Amelia Jane had a wonderful idea. 'My butterfly-net!' she cried. 'My net! I can catch them like fish!'

She stood on the bank and put her big net into the river. She slipped it under the toy soldier. She caught him and dragged him to the shore. She tipped him out safely and then put her net in again. She caught the golden-haired doll, and dragged her out, dripping wet.

Then she fished for the pink rabbit and the clockwork mouse, and caught them both together.

Out they came, gasping and spluttering, on to the bank.

'Oh, Amelia, thank you!' cried the toys, hugging her. 'Oh, you've saved them all! We *are* glad you brought your net with you, even though you caught us like butterflies. But it's been so useful, and you've been so good! Oh, Amelia, you are so very naughty and so very good too!'

'Can I go back to the nursery with you, please?' asked Amelia Jane humbly.

'Of course, of course!' cried the toys. 'Get on to the boiler of the engine, Amelia. You shall drive. We must hurry back and dry the poor wet toys, or they will get dreadful colds. Hurry, hurry!'

So off they all went back to the nursery again, and Amelia Jane's butterfly-net was stuck, dripping wet, into the funnel, where it looked even more peculiar than before. But nobody minded. And Amelia Jane was very happy. She had been good and the toys loved her after all. She really did feel pleased!

Amelia Jane and the Pig

Once, when naughty Amelia Jane was poking about in the toy-cupboard, she found an old balloon-pig, quite flat.

You've seen those balloon-pigs, haven't you? You blow them up like balloons, and they stand on four funny little legs, have a squiggly tail and a nose that you blow into to make the pig fat. And when they go down they make a dreadful wailing noise.

Well, as soon as Amelia Jane saw that balloon-pig, she was *very* pleased! Now she could play a fine trick on the toys.

'I shall make them jump like anything!' she said. 'Oh, won't they be frightened! The toy soldier will run away, and the clown will hide under a chair!'

Amelia Jane took the pig to the dolls' house. There was nobody there. All the toys were looking at a book at the other end of the nursery.

Amelia pushed the pig in through the little front door. It was still flat, so it went in quite easily. Then she put her mouth to its nose and blew. She blew and blew. The pig grew fat. The air inside it blew up its round little body, and it became like a proper little pig.

It stood on its four legs. Its tail stood up nicely. Its tiny, painted eyes looked at Amelia in surprise.

Amelia Jane grinned at the pig. 'You're going to give everyone a dreadful scare when you go down flat!' she said. 'Now mind you squeal and wail at the top of your voice!'

The pig stared at her. It didn't want to go down flat. It liked being a fat, round pig.

Amelia took her thumb away from the pig's snout. Air began to escape from it at once – and the pig began to make that strange wailing noise that all balloon-pigs make.

'Eeeee-oooow-eeeee, oooooo-ooh!' What a dreadful noise it made!

Amelia Jane hid inside the toy-cupboard and watched what would happen. The clockwork clown fell down flat with surprise.

Tom ran away and fell over a brick, bang! on to his nose. The clockwork mouse shot into the golden-haired doll and upset her on the floor. What a disturbance there was!

'What's that? What's that?' cried the teddy bear, looking all round.

'Somebody's in trouble! Somebody is wailing for help! Quick, quick, what is it?'

'Perhaps it's Amelia Jane making that awful noise,' said the clown, looking round.

Amelia Jane stuck her head out of the toy-cupboard. 'Well, it's not me!' she said. 'It must be the Tiddley-Widdley-Wonkies! They always make a noise like that!'

The toys had never heard of the Tiddley-Widdley-Wonkies before – and no wonder, because Amelia Jane had made the name up just that very minute. The toys looked at one

another in horror.

'The Tiddley-Widdley-Wonkies!' said the
teddy bear. 'What are they? Why do they
make that awful noise?'

'Eeeeeee-oooooo-ow-ooooo-eeeeh!'
wailed the balloon-pig in the dolls' house.

The toys clutched one another and went pale. This was dreadful.

'Will the Tiddley-Widdley-Wonkies eat us?' asked the poor little clockwork mouse, trembling so much that his tail shook like a catkin on a tree.

'Oh, of course, if they get you!' said Amelia Jane, enjoying herself very much. 'Look out! They may come for you any minute!'

'Eeeee-oooo-ow-ooooooh!' wailed the pig, slowly getting flatter as he squealed. The toys rushed to the toy-cupboard and clambered in, trembling.

'I d-d-d-don't like the Tiddley-Widdley-Wonkies,' wept the clockwork mouse, who was always easily frightened.

'Well, I'll tell them to go, then,' said Amelia Jane grandly.

She knew that the pig must be almost flat by now, and would soon stop squealing. So she went out of the cupboard and called loudly: 'Tiddley-Widdley-Wonkies! Go away at once, or I, Amelia Jane, will come after you and get you!'

'Eeeeeeeeeeeeeeeeh!' said the pig in the dolls' house, and then said no more. He was quite flat now – not a scrap of air was left inside him.

There was silence. 'There you are!' said Amelia Jane. 'The Tiddley-Widdley-Wonkies are afraid of me. They've gone!'

'Oh, thank you, Amelia Jane!' cried all the toys. 'That *was* brave of you!'

Amelia Jane giggled away to herself all that night, whenever she thought of the squealing pig. She made up her naughty little mind to play the same trick again the very next night.

So when she saw that the toys were busy playing at the other end of the nursery, she went over to the dolls' house again, and put her hand in at the window to pick up the flat balloon-pig. She got hold of his nose and began to blow air into him.

Now the clockwork mouse happened to be in the dolls' house that night. He had curled himself up in one of the cots there, as he sometimes did when he was tired. But Amelia Jane didn't know that. He was in the bedroom just above the room where the balloon-pig was.

Well, Amelia Jane blew and blew till the balloon-pig was fat. Then she ran off to the toy-cupboard again and listened to the pig beginning to wail, 'Eeeeeeeee-ooooooh!'

'It's the Tiddley-Widdley-Wonkies again!' yelled the clown. 'Come on and hide, everybody!'

They ran to hide, and then found that the clockwork mouse was not with them. Where was he?

Well, he was in the dolls' house as you know – and, dear me, how frightened he was when he heard that dreadful wailing noise in the room below him! He jumped out of the cot, and ran downstairs to escape.

But he couldn't escape because the balloon-pig was so fat and big that he blocked the front door. The mouse couldn't get out, and he was just about to run back upstairs in fright, when he saw that it was the pig who was making the noise.

'It's not the Tiddley-Widdley-Wonkies

69

then!' said the mouse to himself. 'It's just that old balloon-pig, and I guess it's Amelia Jane who's blown him up, too, just to give us a fright – the bad doll!'

The clockwork mouse found a pin that was pinning up the curtains. He dug it into the balloon-pig.

Pop! The pig burst.

'I've killed the Tiddley-Widdley-Wonkies!
I've killed the Tiddley-Widdley-Wonkies!'
cried the little mouse, rushing out of the front
door in delight.

'What! What! How did you do it?' cried all
the toys, running up.

Proudly the mouse showed them the flat pig.

The toys stared and stared.

'That's Amelia Jane again,' said the clown
in a rage. 'Frightening us all like that!'

'Let's give *her* a scare too,' said the bear.
'Can't we think of something that will make a
noise and frighten her dreadfully? It's just no
good letting her do these things to us.'

'Well, what noise can we make?' said the
golden-haired doll. They all thought hard.

'If I rub my paw hard against the windowpane it makes a fine squeaky noise,' said the bear.

'And if I get the slate out of the cupboard and press hard on it with a pencil, it makes a terrible squeal,' said Tom, grinning.

'And if I get that old broken violin out of the chest there, and pull its one string, it goes "Plooonk! Plooonk!" just like that,' said the clown. 'I saw one of the children doing it the other day.'

'Well, we'll do all that,' said the doll, pleased. So the clown went to get the old violin. It still had just one string. The clown hid it behind the coal-scuttle, and waited there.

The teddy bear climbed up to the window-sill and hid behind the curtain. Tom got the old slate out of the cupboard, found a broken slate-pencil, and hid it under the table behind the cushion there.

Now they would wait until Amelia came by.

Amelia was looking at the pig in the dolls' house, wondering if she could mend him. She felt very angry with the mouse for spoiling her joke. The mouse watched her. It was his job to make Amelia Jane run near the coal-scuttle, the window, and the table if he could so that the toys could make their noises.

'You wait till I catch you, you naughty little mouse!' cried Amelia.

'Can't catch me, can't catch me!' squeaked the mouse joyfully, and ran off. Amelia Jane ran after him. He ran by the window. The teddy bear ran his paw up and down at once. 'Eeeeeeh! Eeeeeeeh! Eeeeeeh!'

'Oh! what's that?' cried Amelia in a fright.

She ran under the table – but Tom was
waiting there with his slate and pencil.
He rubbed the pencil hard up and down
the slate. What a terrible squealing it made!
Amelia jumped as if she had been shot,
and ran straight into the table-leg, bump!

'Ow-ee, ow-ee, ow-ee!' went the slate

pencil. Amelia Jane rushed away, and saw
the mouse grinning at her from behind the
coal-scuttle. She ran after him in a great
rage. She didn't know that the
clown was there with the old
violin! He pulled the
string a good
many times.

'Plooooonk!
Ploooonk! Plooooonk!'
growled the violin.

'Oh! Who's hiding
there? Who's
growling at me?'
yelled poor Amelia.

'It's the Tiddley-Widdley-Wonkies, of
course,' shouted all the toys in delight. 'Look
out, Amelia Jane, look out!'

Amelia Jane rushed into the cupboard, shut the door, and shivered. Were there really Tiddley-Widdley-Wonkies after all? Oh dear, oh dear, oh dear!

And there she stayed for two whole nights and wouldn't go out to play! Poor Amelia Jane!

Amelia Jane is Terribly Naughty

Once Amelia Jane, the big naughty doll, discovered a tiny hole in the quilt on the dolls' cot. So she poked her finger inside and pulled out a feather. She threw it up into the air.

'Look!' she shouted. 'This quilt is full of feathers. Did you know there were feathers in quilts, Toys?'

'Amelia Jane! Don't pull out any more feathers!' said Tom at once, seeing the big doll pull out two more.

'Oh, I must, I must,' said Amelia, and she tore the hole a little more till it was quite a big one. Then she could put in her hand – and out came dozens of feathers!

'I shall make a snowstorm, a snowstorm, a snowstorm!' sang Amelia Jane in delight. She climbed up on to the nursery table and began to shake the quilt. Well, as you can imagine, out flew hundreds and hundreds of white feathers! Amelia Jane became very excited.

'I'm making snow, I'm making snow!' she shouted. 'Come out in the snowstorm, Toys!'

The toys stared at the naughty doll in dismay. What a mess she was making! Whatever were they to do?

The feathers flew all about the room, floating lightly in the air, and it really did look rather like a snowstorm.

Amelia Jane got another quilt – and she made a hole at one end.

She climbed up to the table again and shook the quilt. Out flew hundreds more feathers!

She squealed with delight. 'You'll soon be able to make a snowman, Toys!'

'Don't be silly, Amelia Jane,' said the clockwork clown. 'I simply can't think how you can be so naughty.'

'Oh, it's quite easy,' said bad Amelia Jane, and she shook twenty feathers down on to the clockwork clown's head. The clockwork mouse watched from a corner. He really felt a bit afraid of so many feathers.

'I wonder where there is another quilt,' said Amelia Jane, who never could stop, once she had begun. 'Oh, I believe I know where there is an old cushion. That will be full of feathers too. I think I saw one of the children put it on the top shelf of the nursery cupboard. I'll climb up and see.'

She went to the cupboard, walking through

the cloud of feathers. She blew them away as she went. It was fun. She came to the cupboard and opened the door. In the cupboard were many shelves, for a great deal was kept there – the nursery cups and saucers were there, the knives and forks, the treacle for the porridge, the honey, the jam, a tin of biscuits, mending things – and on the top shelf was a collection of things that needed sewing – a cushion with a hole in, a teacloth, and a tablecloth.

Amelia Jane began to climb up the shelves – and then a dreadful thing happened. She caught hold

of the saucer in which the tin of treacle stood
– and it tipped up at once. The lid came off
– the treacle tin lost its balance and fell
straight on Amelia Jane's head. The treacle
trickled down all over her.

'Ooooh, Amelia Jane! Now look what
you've done,' shouted the toys, as they saw
the treacle dripping down all over the big
doll.

'Oh, I don't like it! It's sticky!' cried Amelia
Jane, and she jumped down from the
cupboard.

And then a funny thing happened. The
feathers, which were still floating all over the
room, fell on to the sticky treacle – and before
you could say, 'Look at Amelia Jane!' she was
covered with feathers!

The toys began to laugh. They simply

couldn't help it. First Amelia was covered
with treacle, and then with feathers – and it
was all because of her own naughtiness!

'*Don't* laugh at me, you horrid things!'
yelled Amelia in a temper, and she ran at the
toys. But the more she ran through the
feathers, the more they stuck to her – and at

last she looked like a strange and peculiar bird!

The toys laughed till they couldn't laugh any more. Amelia Jane got angrier and angrier, and tried to tear off the feathers. Then she lay down on the floor and rolled about to get them off – but she forgot that there were hundreds of feathers on the carpet, so when she got up there were more stuck to her than ever!

'It's the funniest sight I've ever seen,' said Tom, wiping his eyes, for he had laughed till he cried. Amelia Jane flew at the toy soldier. Then she ran at the teddy bear and the frightened clockwork mouse. She was a big doll and the toys were really terrified, but Amelia wouldn't stop.

'*I'll* teach you to laugh at me!' she cried.

And then something happened to Amelia. The door of the nursery opened softly, and in walked the big black kitchen cat. When he saw Amelia Jane covered in feathers, he stopped and stared.

'What! A *bird* in the nursery!' he mewed. 'I'll catch it for my dinner!'

Then it was Amelia's turn to be frightened. She ran into a corner and hid there. 'No, don't catch me, don't catch me!' she cried. 'I'm Amelia Jane!'

'Rubbish!' said the cat. 'You've got feathers growing on you – dolls don't have feathers! I shall catch you, you most peculiar bird!'

He crept quietly up to the corner. Amelia gave a squeal and ran away. She hid behind the brick-box. The cat followed again, and crouched down, ready to spring.

Amelia yelled for help.

'Toys! Save me! Save me! Quick, come and help me!'

But the toys thought it was time that Amelia was punished. Now she must see what it was like to be chased and hurt.

The cat sprang. He landed right on Amelia Jane and squashed all the breath out of her. He dug his claws into her and scratched her.

She squealed and squealed.

He sniffed at her in disgust and then jumped away. He couldn't bear the sticky treacle on his paws. He licked them clean and then walked out of the nursery with his tail in the air.

'You're only a doll after all,' he said. 'Well, if you dress yourself up in feathers and treacle, you must expect trouble!'

Amelia Jane cried so much that the toys came round to comfort her. She had had her punishment, and they were too kind-hearted to keep away any longer.

'Now listen to me, Amelia,' said Tom sternly. 'We will wash the treacle off you – but after that you must see to the feathers. You must pick up every single one and stuff them all back into the quilts, and sew up the holes. Do you hear?'

'Yes, Tom,' said Amelia Jane in a small voice. So they took her to the basin and washed away the treacle. It made her very wet and she had to dry herself by the fire. Then she had to pick up all the feathers. Nobody helped her, because, as the toy soldier said, she really had to learn that she must pay for being naughty.

Then Amelia Jane put the feathers back and sewed up the holes in the quilts. 'I've done all you said,' she said in a sorry sort of voice. 'I won't be bad again.'

But nobody believed her – and I don't expect you do either!

Amelia Jane is Tired

Once Amelia Jane, the big naughty doll, went out walking with the teddy bear. They went to the shops and Amelia Jane spent fifty pence. She bought a little watering can, and the teddy bear wasn't at all pleased.

'I suppose you'll use that to water the toys, instead of watering flowers,' he said. 'Well – I shall buy something really sensible. I want an umbrella.'

'An *umbrella*!' said Amelia Jane with a giggle. 'What do you want an umbrella for?'

'Well, it might rain, mightn't it?' said the teddy bear, in a huff.

'There isn't a cloud in the sky and the sun is

shining brightly,' said Amelia Jane. 'But still, if you think it will rain out of a blue sky, you'd certainly better buy the umbrella, Teddy.'

The bear had seen a really lovely umbrella. It was bright red, and had a beautiful handle made of red glass. The bear asked how much it was, and was very delighted when he found that he had enough money to pay for it.

He bought it, and proudly set off home with it. It really looked very nice indeed. Amelia Jane half wished *she* had bought an umbrella too. But still, she liked her green watering can, and planned all sorts of tricks with it.

They lost their way and walked about a mile before they came to a place they knew. Amelia Jane felt tired. She told the bear.

'Teddy, please give me a piggy-back home,' she said. 'I'm too tired to walk any further.'

'Well! I like *that*!' said the bear, surprised. 'Give you a piggy-back home when I'm very tired myself? I should think not indeed! You can walk home on your own feet.'

'Oh, *do* give me a piggy-back,' begged Amelia. But the bear said no, and no, and no.

91

Three times he said it, each time more loudly
than the last. Then he sat down below a tree
and yawned.

'I must just have a rest,' he said. 'Sit quietly,
now, Amelia. Don't disturb me.'

Amelia Jane frowned at the bear. Then,
when she saw that he had shut his eyes, she
smiled. She stole off to a little stream nearby
and filled her green watering can. Then she
quietly climbed the tree above the teddy bear
and sat on a low-hanging branch there,
hidden in the leaves.

She tipped up the can. A shower of little
cold drops went down on the bear. He
opened his eyes in a hurry.

'Amelia! Oh, Amelia, it's beginning to
rain!' he cried gladly. 'Now I can use my
lovely new umbrella!'

Amelia emptied a few more drops down. The bear was simply delighted. He put up his new red umbrella at once, smiling with joy. To think that it should rain the very first time he had his new umbrella.

Amelia emptied the rest of the water on to the umbrella. It made a pitter-pattering sound that pleased the bear very much. He listened to it, with his head on one side.

Amelia carefully let herself down from the tree-branch and sat on top of the red umbrella, holding on to the little stick that stuck up from the bottom. The bear didn't know anything about Amelia doing this, for he couldn't see through the umbrella!

He thought that his umbrella was very heavy, though. Still, that made him rather proud.

That's the umbrella getting wet, I suppose, he thought. The rain is wetting it and making it heavy. What a fine umbrella it is. Then he looked round for Amelia.

'Amelia Jane! Where are you? I'm going home. You can share my umbrella with me if you like, so that you don't get wet.'

Amelia Jane grinned. She was sharing the umbrella all right – and she wasn't getting wet either! She didn't say a word.

'Well, I suppose she's gone home by herself,' said the bear, and he got up. His umbrella did feel heavy! Never mind – it showed it was a good one. He walked off down the lane, carrying it carefully, not noticing that it wasn't raining at all!

He got back to the nursery, and the toys were *most* surprised to see the umbrella up

– with Amelia Jane on top of it! They crowded round in astonishment.

'Hallo!' said the bear. 'See my new umbrella? Isn't it fine? Is Amelia Jane home yet? Do you know, she wanted me to *carry* her home! I said no, no, NO. As if I would dream of carrying that great fat doll home. The idea!'

The toys giggled. The bear frowned at them. 'What are you giggling at?' he asked. 'Surely you are not giggling at my fine new umbrella?'

'No – we are giggling because you said you wouldn't carry Amelia Jane home – and you have!' laughed the clockwork clown.

'I have not,' said the bear crossly.

'You have!' cried Amelia Jane, and she thumped on the top of the umbrella. 'I'm here!'

The bear let down his umbrella at once –
and Amelia Jane slipped to the ground as it
shut. The bear stared at her in a rage, and
Amelia Jane stared back.

'You bad doll,' said the bear. 'No wonder
my umbrella felt heavy. You might have
broken it. How dare you make me carry you
when I said I wouldn't!'

'Oh, I like getting my own way,' said
Amelia Jane, and she laughed and laughed.

But then she found that she had left behind
her nice little new watering can! She had left
it in the tree. She *was* upset. 'Oh, please, will
someone go back and fetch it for me?' she
cried.

But nobody would. 'What! Fetch a
watering can that you only bought because
you thought you could play tricks on us with

it!' cried the sailor doll. 'I should think not indeed. We'll leave the can there for somebody else to find – and serve you right too, Amelia Jane!'

So the little green can is still up the tree, and nobody has found it yet. Wouldn't it be fun if *you* did!

A Shock for Amelia Jane

Amelia Jane had no manners at all. She was the biggest doll in the nursery, and you might have thought she would be the best behaved. But she wasn't.

Whenever other toys paid a visit to the nursery they were always shocked by Amelia Jane. She never shook hands and said how-do-you-do. She never said goodbye nicely. And she never offered visiting toys any sweets, even if she had some.

So you can guess that the toys who lived with Amelia Jane were ashamed of her.

'When Peter brought his toy soldier the other day, Amelia Jane squirted him with the water pistol,' said the clockwork clown.

'And when Betsy-May brought her best doll for a visit, Amelia Jane dabbed her with a paint-brush and made her nose all blue,' said the teddy bear.

'Yes, but the worst thing she ever did was to make a hole in that floating duck that Billy-Bob brought to show our children,' said the clockwork mouse.

'She poked it with a pin – and it filled with water and sank. That was a very bad thing to do.'

'I wish we could teach her manners,' said the teddy bear.

'So do I,' said the golden-haired doll, who had most beautiful manners herself, and always said 'thank you' and 'please' at the right moments.

The clockwork mouse began to giggle.

He had a funny giggle that went on and on, and it made the other toys giggle too.

'What's the matter?' asked Tom.

'I've got a little idea,' said the mouse, quivering his rubber tail.

'Can't we dress something up, and pretend it is someone come to see if we've got manners, and give Amelia Jane a shock?'

'But what could we dress up?' asked the golden-haired doll. 'I don't see what you mean.'

'Well, listen,' said the clockwork mouse. 'You know that balloon in the cupboard, don't you? Let's paint a face on it, and stick some hairs on, and put a hat on it. Then one of us could wrap a coat and a shawl round our shoulders and head and pretend that the balloon-face is our face – and we could come

103

visiting the nursery and pretend to be very shocked at Amelia's manners.'

'Yes – it might be a good idea,' said the clown. 'It would certainly be very funny. We'll try it! And oh, I say! We'll tell Amelia Jane that it's Mrs Good-Manners come to visit us, and that she'll burst with rage if she finds any of us without good manners – and we'll stick a pin into her head at the back when Amelia is being rude to her, to make her really burst. Oh, what a shock for Amelia Jane!'

The toys began to giggle again. Amelia Jane had gone out in the pram with the children, so they had plenty of time to do what they wanted to. The clown ran to the cupboard and took out the balloon. He blew it up till it was nice and round.

The teddy bear got the paintbox and painted rather a fierce sort of face on the balloon. Tom begged the rocking-horse for some hairs out of his tail and stuck them on to the balloon-face for hair. Then the toys found an old doll's hat with flowers in, and put that on the balloon-head. It did look funny.

'*I'll* be Mrs Good-Manners,' said the teddy bear, who was nice and plump. He giggled. 'This is going to be funny. I shall love being Mrs Good-Manners! Get me an old dress and a shawl, and some doll's boots for my feet.'

Very soon the bear was all dressed up, and the toys tied the balloon-neck to the shawl that went over his head. He really looked as if the balloon-face was his own face – it was very funny.

The bear put on a most polite kind of voice and walked round the nursery curtseying and bowing to everyone.

'Good-day! *Good*-day! I hope I see you well? And how do you do, *dear* Mister Clockwork Clown? How is your dear mother? Oh, and here is *dear* little Clockwork Mouse. How are you, my pet?'

Everyone squealed with laughter to see the big balloon-face with its old hat on top, waggling round at everyone as the bear trotted about the nursery. The mouse couldn't say a word because he was laughing so much. Even his tail seemed to laugh and got all curled up.

'Oh, you're lovely, Teddy!' cried Tom. 'Now listen – you act just like this when Amelia Jane comes, won't you – and be very, very shocked if she's rude – and after a bit I'll creep behind you with a pin and dig it into your balloon-head without Amelia noticing. And then what a shock she will get!'

Just then the children came back, and Amelia Jane was with them. The toys scurried into the toy-cupboard – all except the bear, and he slipped out into the passage and hid in the broom-cupboard there.

 107

Well, when the nursery was empty again, and the children had gone to their rest, there came a knock at the door.

'Who's that?' said Amelia in surprise.

'I think it's Mrs Good-Manners come to pay us a visit,' said Tom. 'I did hear she was going round the nurseries to make sure that toys knew their manners.'

'Oh, really?' said Amelia in surprise. 'What a silly person she must be! *I* shan't be polite to her.'

'You must be, Amelia Jane,' said Tom. 'She may be very cross if you are not.'

The knocking came again. The clown went across the nursery and opened the door. In walked the bear, dressed up as Mrs Good-Manners, with his balloon-head waggling about.

'Good-day!' said
Mrs Good-
Manners, going
across to the
clockwork clown.
'And how do
you do?'

'Very well, thank
you,' answered the
clown politely,
'and how are you?'

'Well, I thank you,' answered Mrs Good-
Manners. Then she turned to Amelia Jane
and held out her hand.

'And how are you, Amelia Jane?' she asked.

'Oh, I've got earache in my toes and
toothache in my knee,' said Amelia very
rudely, and she wouldn't shake hands.

'What bad manners!' said Mrs Good-Manners, shocked. 'You make me feel quite faint.'

'I'll throw some cold water over you then. That will make you feel better!' said Amelia Jane.

'Pray do no such thing,' said Mrs Good-Manners hurriedly. 'Amelia, you are a very rude doll. I must insist that you learn better manners.'

'Insist all you like,' said Amelia rudely. 'I think good manners are just silly. Now do go away. We don't want you in our nursery!'

'Amelia Jane, you are making me very cross!' said Mrs Good-Manners in a fierce voice, and her head waggled about in a rather alarming manner. Amelia felt a little uncomfortable. She had never seen anyone with such a waggly head before.

'Oh, go away!' said the naughty doll. 'I'm tired of you!'

'Amelia! You will make Mrs Good-Manners burst with rage!' cried Tom, running up. 'Be careful! She is getting angrier and angrier.'

'*She* won't burst with rage!' said Amelia. 'People never do!'

'I'm going to burst! I know I am!' said Mrs Good-Manners in a fierce voice. 'I'm going to burst with rage!'

Tom slyly dug his pin into the back of Mrs Good-Manners' balloon-head.

BANG! It burst – and suddenly Mrs Good-Manners had no head at all. Amelia Jane gave a scream.

'Oh! She *has* burst! I've killed her with my bad manners and rudeness! Oh! Oh!'

111

The bear fell down on the ground as soon as he heard the balloon burst – so it looked as if Mrs Good-Manners had tumbled flat. The toys, trying to hide their giggles, all ran up.

'Oh, you wicked doll, Amelia! You've made poor Mrs Good-Manners burst with rage!'

'I didn't mean to, I didn't mean to,' wept Amelia, who was now most alarmed.

'Poor, poor Mrs Good-Manners!' said the clockwork mouse. 'Now that's the end of her.'

'Oh, don't say things like that!' wept Amelia.

'You are a very bad doll to make people burst with rage at your rudeness,' said Tom sternly. 'Go and stand in the corner with your back to us for half an hour. We don't want to look at you.'

Amelia Jane
was so frightened
and sorry that she
very humbly went
into the corner
and stood there,
sniffing and
crying. The toys
quickly took the
boots, shawl, and

frock off the giggling teddy bear and threw
them into the cupboard. They put the burst
balloon-head into the wastepaper basket.

'Now we'll make a bargain with Amelia
Jane,' whispered the bear. He cleared his
throat, and spoke to Amelia.

'Amelia! Do you feel sorry for what you
did? What are you going to do about it?'

 113

'Oh, I do feel sorry, I do, I do,' sobbed Amelia. 'And I don't know *what* to do about it! Please, please don't tell anyone I've made Mrs Good-Manners burst with rage.'

'Well, suppose we keep the secret for you – are you going to behave better in future?' asked Tom sternly.

'Oh, much, much better,' said Amelia, wiping her eyes. 'I'll always say please and thank you and how-do-you-do – really I will!'

'Very well – you can come out of the corner and we'll give you another chance,' said Tom. 'We will never tell anyone what you've done.'

So Amelia came out of the corner and stared round to find Mrs Good-Manners. But she was gone, of course – and Amelia Jane never found out what had happened to her.

But – my goodness, what a difference there was in Amelia Jane's manners after that! You'd never have known she was the same doll. But how long it will last nobody knows.

Amelia Jane's Hair Goes Flat!

One day Amelia Jane quarrelled with the clockwork clown, who was playing with the picture-bricks very nicely and quietly all by himself in a corner. He was making a picture of some hens in a farmyard, and was turning each brick over and over to find bits of hens to fit into his picture.

Along came Amelia Jane and looked at the half-made picture. 'I'll help you,' she said.

'I don't want any help, thank you,' said the clockwork clown very politely. 'I like making pictures all by myself.'

'Don't be mean,' said Amelia, who did love poking her nose into what other people were doing. 'Let me help. Look – that brick shouldn't be there; I'm sure it shouldn't. It should be over here.'

She took hold of a brick that the clown had neatly fitted into place and put it somewhere else. It was quite wrong. The clockwork clown glared at Amelia.

'It should *not* be there,' he said, and put it back into its place.

'I tell you it should,' said Amelia, and she picked it up again. 'Look – that bit of hen's tail goes on to this bit of brown body.'

'Amelia Jane, you're wrong, and even if you were right I wouldn't want you to help,' said the clown crossly. 'I do like making pictures by myself. Go away.'

'Shan't!' said Amelia Jane.

'You jolly well will!' said the clown angrily. 'I'll push you to the other side of the nursery.'

'You couldn't. I'm too big,' said Amelia.

This was quite true. Amelia Jane was far too big to push. So the clockwork clown turned his back on her, said something rude under his breath, and went on with his brick picture by himself. Amelia Jane was angry.

'If you don't let me help, I'll throw all your bricks out of the window!' she said.

'You won't!' cried the clown, in horror.

'I just will!' shouted Amelia, quite losing her temper. And do you know, she picked up two bricks and threw them straight out of the window!

The clown was angry and dismayed. His lovely bricks! Now he couldn't make his picture. He was so cross that he picked up a brick and threw it straight at Amelia Jane.

Then, as you can imagine, Amelia went quite mad. She picked up all the bricks one by one and threw them right out of the window! Not one was left. The clown and the rest of the toys stared at Amelia in horror. What would the children say when they found all their lovely picture-bricks out on the grass?

'Look!' cried the clown suddenly. 'It's beginning to rain! Just look!'

So it was. The first big raindrops began to come down, splish-splash. Amelia Jane went rather red. She knew that rain spoilt things.

'It's going to pour, simply *pour*!' said the teddy bear. 'And I know what's going to happen to those bricks. The paper on them, that makes the pretty picture, is going to get soaking wet and peel off. Then there won't be any picture. That's what's going to happen.'

'Oh, Amelia Jane! It is *tire*some of you!' said Tom. 'Just because you lost your temper with the clown you spoil all the lovely bricks. You deserve to be punished.'

For once in a way Amelia Jane was ashamed of herself. She liked the picture-bricks, and had often made the hen-picture, the dog-picture, and the rabbit-picture. Now they would all be spoilt.

'I'll go out and bring in the bricks!' she cried suddenly. 'Yes, I will. I'm sorry I threw them out now, but I didn't know it was going to rain!'

'You'll get soaked!' cried the bear. But Amelia didn't listen. She ran to the door and down the passage to the stairs.

'Amelia! At least put something over your head!' cried the clown.

But Amelia wasn't going to stop for anything. She never did! Down the stairs she ran and into the garden. And my word, how the rain did pelt down! The raindrops hit Amelia Jane very hard, almost as if they were smacking her!

'Don't!' cried Amelia – but they didn't stop, of course, and Amelia couldn't fight raindrops. She ran to the bricks and began to pick them up as fast as she could. They

kept tumbling out of her arms, and she had to pick them all up again. The rain went on and on pouring down, and soaked Amelia Jane from head to foot. All the bounce came out of her hair and it hung down like rats' tails!

At last Amelia had all the bricks and she went indoors again. When she came into the nursery the toys cried out in horror: 'Amelia Jane! You are dripping wet!'

'Yes,' said poor Amelia, 'and I do feel cold and horrid. Here are the bricks. They are rather wet too. What are we going to do with them?'

'I'll put them into the hot-cupboard on the landing and let them dry slowly,' said Tom. 'Help me, Bear. And you had better take off your wet things, Amelia, and put on a nightie or something, so that your clothes can be dried in the hot-cupboard too.'

Whilst the toy soldier was taking the bricks to the hot-cupboard, Amelia Jane took off her wet things. She put on her nightie and a coat, and felt a bit warmer. The bear took her wet clothes to be dried in the hot-cupboard.

'What about your hair?' asked the clown, feeling it. 'Goodness! Isn't it wet! And all the bounce has come out, Amelia. It looks awfully flat and funny!'

'Perhaps the bounce will come back when it's dry,' said Amelia anxiously. 'Get a towel, Clown, and help me to dry it.'

So the clown, the toy soldier, the other dolls, the bear, and even the clockwork mouse all took a turn at rubbing Amelia's wet hair. Soon it was quite dry and Amelia brushed it out. But alas! It was now as straight and as flat as a poker, without a single wave anywhere! The rain had spoilt all the bounciness.

Amelia Jane cried. 'I have been asked to a party tomorrow. The children were taking me with them to Judy's birthday party. And I can't possibly go with hair like this.

I look such a fright! Oh dear, I do wish I hadn't thrown those bricks out of the window like that! Then I wouldn't have needed to go out in the rain and get them.'

The toys really felt sorry for Amelia. She didn't look a bit like herself, sitting there with straight, flat hair and a very miserable face.

'Well, Amelia, you were very silly,' said the bear at last. 'But it's a pity if you have to have two punishments for one silliness – having your hair all straight and missing a party too! I wonder if we could curl it for you. How is hair curled, I wonder?'

'In curlers,' said Tom. 'A little girl once came to stay the night here and I saw her nanny putting her hair in curlers.'

So the toys hunted for curlers but they couldn't find any at all, which was not

 127

surprising, for there were none in the house. Then the clockwork mouse had an idea.

'What about curl-papers?' he squeaked. 'I know people sometimes use bits of paper to twist hair up in, and we could do that to Amelia Jane.'

So they hunted for an old newspaper, or paper of any sort – but there wasn't a piece to be found at all! Amelia Jane was quite in despair.

Then the clown looked into the toy-cupboard and saw the kite lying there, with its long tail made of twisted bits of paper.

'Look!' he cried. 'Just the very thing! Kite, may we borrow your tail, please? We will put all the papers back tomorrow.'

Well, the kite had seen how Amelia had run out into the rain to get the bricks, so he was quite willing for his tail to be used. The toys spent a long time untying the twists of paper that made his tail, but at last they had finished. And then they had some fun twisting Amelia Jane's long straight hair up in the bits of paper. Soon, she looked very funny indeed, with curl-papers all over her head!

'There! It won't be long before your hair is all nice and curly again!' cried the clown.

Amelia Jane kept the curl-papers in for a long time. In fact, she wouldn't take them out – and the children came into the nursery the next afternoon to look for her to take her to the party! *How* astonished they were to see Amelia Jane with curl-papers all over her head!

'Goodness, Amelia, who put those in?' they cried. 'What a funny sight you look!'

They took the curl-papers out – and you *should* have seen Amelia's hair! It was bouncier than it had ever been before, and when it was well-brushed it *did* look nice.

'You shall wear one of my very own hair-ribbons!' cried one of the children. So Amelia Jane went to the party very happily, wearing a bright red ribbon in her bouncy yellow hair.

'I'll bring you each back a sweet if I can,' she promised the toys. 'You've been really kind to me!'

And what about the curl-papers? Well, the children threw them into the waste-paper basket because, you see, they didn't know that they had come off the tail of the kite! But the toys took them out of the basket, and, long before the children and Amelia Jane came back, they had tied the papers on to the tail of the kite again.

'I guess no other kite has a tail that was used for curl-papers!' cried the kite. And he was right!

Amelia Jane and the
Snow-Doll

Did I ever tell you how Amelia Jane, that big
naughty doll, made herself a snow-baby? She
was really very funny about it.

One afternoon the snow fell thickly. Then it

stopped, and the toys climbed up to the windowsill to look out.

'Isn't the snow pretty?' said the clockwork clown.

'Like a white blanket,' said the toy soldier. 'Let's go and play in it. The children are out, so we can slip into the garden and have some fun.'

'We'll make a snowman!' said the teddy bear.

So out they all went. But Amelia Jane was very tiresome. She would keep snowballing everybody, and as she was big and strong, her snowballs really hurt when they hit anyone. The clockwork mouse cried bitterly when one hit him on the nose.

'I'm sure it's bent my nose,' he sobbed. 'Is my nose bent, Tom?'

'Not a bit,' said Tom. 'And if it was it wouldn't matter. You would look just as sweet. Now, Amelia Jane, stop snowballing and come and help us to make a nice snowman. It's really fun to do that, you know. We are going to give him an old hat belonging to the golden-haired doll, and there's an old scarf we can use, too. Come and help.'

But Amelia wouldn't. She stopped throwing snowballs, though. She watched the toys making the snowman and then she thought of an idea herself.

'I'm going to make a snow-baby,' she said. 'A dear little snow-doll that I can dress up and keep for myself. Much better than a silly old snowman.'

'Well, I do think you might come and help,' said the bear. 'It's much more fun when everyone gives a hand. Don't be selfish, Amelia Jane.'

But Amelia Jane meant to have her own way. She gathered up handfuls of snow, and pressed them together. She made a neat little body and a dear little head. She put tiny stones into the head for eyes and a bit of stick for a mouth.

'Look at my baby snow-doll!' she cried. But the others wouldn't look. They were cross with Amelia.

'Well, don't look then,' said Amelia. 'I shan't look at that silly snowman of yours either. How stupid he is!'

'How do you know he is stupid if you haven't looked at him?' asked the bear cleverly. 'Ha, ha! You must have taken a peep then.'

'I'm going into the nursery to find a few clothes for my darling baby snow-doll,' said Amelia, in a huff. 'She shall be dressed properly — not wear just a hat and scarf like your silly snowman.'

She went indoors. She found a dear little blue frock and a petticoat. She dragged a blue bonnet out of the doll's chest of drawers,

and found a red coat. Now her snow-baby
would look fine!

She went outside again and dressed the
snow-doll. It wasn't at all easy, and Amelia
Jane had to give up trying to get on the
petticoat because it was too tight. But she
managed to put on the dress and coat – and
the little blue bonnet looked sweet!

'Look, Toys, look at my snow-doll!' cried Amelia Jane, proud of what she had done.

'You wouldn't look at our snowman so we shan't look at your doll,' said the bear. 'That's quite fair, Amelia Jane.'

'Well, I still think your snowman is silly and stupid, even without looking at him,' said Amelia. 'You can't even take him indoors with you. But I am going to take my dear little doll into the nursery with me, and keep her for a pet.'

The toys laughed. 'You are just as silly as you think our snowman is!' said Tom.

Well, the toys went indoors, and had to leave their fine snowman out in the garden, of course. He looked lovely with the old hat and scarf on. But Amelia Jane carried her baby snow-doll into the nursery, and looked at her lovingly. She was really very proud of her.

Amelia got into the toy-cupboard. She felt sleepy after her play in the snow.

'My snow-baby and I are going to have a little snooze,' she said to the toys. 'Please don't disturb us.'

'We wouldn't dream of it!' said Tom, with a grin.

Amelia Jane held her baby snow-doll tightly in her arms and shut her eyes. In half a second she was fast asleep.

'Look!' whispered the teddy bear. 'Amelia's snow-doll is melting because the nursery is warm. Had we better wake her up?'

'No. She said she didn't want to be disturbed,' said the clown. 'Leave her. See what she says when she wakes up!

She will have a horrid shock!'

Well, Amelia Jane slept for an hour – and then she began having horrid dreams about falling into a river and getting cold and wet. She woke up with a jump – and oh, my goodness, whatever had happened? She was clasping a few wet clothes tightly to her – and she was soaked through and dripping wet! The snow-doll had disappeared.

'Oh!' cried Amelia, jumping up, startled. 'What has happened? I'm wet all over! Who has been watering me? Oh, you bad toys, standing laughing there – what have you done with my darling snow-baby? I am dripping wet. I shall get a cold. A-tish-oo!'

Well, nobody would tell Amelia what had happened, but all the toys laughed. Amelia had to go and dry herself by the fire, and she was very cross indeed.

Well, she thought, I do wonder what happened? Could my baby doll have melted and made me wet? Oh, I do hope that silly snowman out in the garden has melted too!

She went to look. He was still there, as grand as could be and he laughed when he saw poor wet Amelia Jane!

'You've looked at me after all!' he seemed to say. 'Don't you think I look fine, Amelia Jane?'

But all Amelia said was, 'A-tish-oo!'

Amelia Jane is Naughty Again!

I'm going to tell you how naughty Amelia Jane, the big bad doll in the nursery, let the canary out of the cage.

There was a dear little canary in the nursery called Goldie. He hopped about from perch to perch and sang a merry carol of a song to the toys. They all loved him very much indeed, and when he dropped seeds out of his cage on to the floor, they collected them in a little pot from the dolls' house and saved them in case they could ever give them back to him.

Now one day Amelia Jane thought she would like to look right into Goldie's cage

and see the water-dish he had there, and the
seed-dish, and the saucer he used for a bath.

So she got a chair and put it just under the
cage. Then she climbed up the chair, and
balanced herself very cleverly on the back.
She caught hold of the side of the cage and
pulled herself up to peep inside.

'Oh!' she said. 'Goldie has a dear little blue saucer for a bath. Goldie, do bath yourself so I can watch!'

So the canary bathed himself and sent silvery drops of water all over Amelia Jane. She laughed and wiped her face.

'Goldie, would you like to fly round the nursery?' said Amelia. 'You could stretch your wings nicely then.'

The toys listened in dismay. 'Amelia Jane! You know that Goldie is not allowed out of his cage unless there is somebody like Nanny or the children in the room to get him back!' cried the clown.

'Oh, I can get him back all right,' said Amelia, and she began to fumble with the catch of the cage-door.

'Amelia Jane! How dare you do such a

 145

thing!' shouted the teddy bear. 'Stop at once! You are not to let Goldie out.'

Well, of course, as soon as Amelia was told she mustn't do a thing she at once felt she must do it. So she slipped back the catch and opened the cage-door. And out hopped Goldie at once in great delight!

He spread his pretty yellow wings and flew all round the room, making quite a wind with them when he passed the watching toys!

'Oh, Goldie! Go back!' cried all the toys. But the little yellow canary didn't mean to! Not he! He had never been free before without the children or somebody in the room – and now he was really going to enjoy himself.

He flew to the top of the clock and sang a little song there. He flew to the mantelpiece

and talked to the china duck that stood there.
He had a really lovely time.

Tom shut the window. The bear pushed the
door till it shut with a click. Then the toys
looked at one another.

'*Now* what are we to do?' said the bear in
despair.

'Tira-tirra-lee!' said the canary from the
top of the toy-cupboard, and cocked his
pretty little head on one side.

Amelia Jane looked inside the cage door.
She wondered what it felt like to be inside

such a nice little cage, with seed on one side, water on the other, the bath on the floor, and a little swing at the top.

'I'll squeeze myself in and see,' said Amelia with a chuckle. So she managed to squeeze herself in through the door, tearing her dress as she did so.

She almost got stuck, for she was a very big doll, but somehow or other she managed to get inside.

'Now I'm a canary!' she shouted to the astonished toys. 'I'm a canary and I'm going to sing!' And she opened her mouth as if it was a beak and tried to sing like Goldie. It was really very funny.

The clockwork clown had an idea. Whilst Amelia Jane was singing he hurriedly climbed up the chair and stood on the back of it,

almost falling off. He just managed to reach
the door – and he shut it and latched it!

'Amelia Jane is caught!' he cried. 'She's shut
in the cage!'

'It serves her right for letting Goldie out!' said the bear. 'Hurrah! Good for you, Clown! See how the bad doll likes being shut up!'

Well, as soon as Amelia found that she was locked in, she didn't like it one bit. She turned to the door and jiggled it hard. But it wouldn't open.

'Let me out!' yelled Amelia, bumping her head against the swing at the top of the cage. 'Let me out! How horrid you all are!'

'You let Goldie out when you shouldn't, and now you've got a good punishment!' said the pink rabbit.

'You be quiet,' said Amelia rudely.

'Clown – Bear – Tom – please, please let me out!'

But the toys were now watching Goldie.

They had heard the cat mewing outside the nursery door and they were afraid. Goldie would certainly be caught if the cat came in – and how dreadful that would be!

'Goldie! Come into the dolls' house,' said the clown suddenly. 'We've got some of your seeds in there in a little dish, and you can eat them. We saved them for you when you scattered them on the floor from your cage.'

Goldie was feeling hungry, so he followed the clown to the pretty dolls' house in the corner. He thought it was a dear little house.

The clown opened the door and went in with the canary. As soon as the yellow bird was safely inside, Tom, who was outside, shut the door with a bang. Now the canary was safe!

The clown took the canary to the kitchen

and opened the little cupboard there. Inside was the little dish of seeds. As soon as the canary was eating them, sitting on a chair at the table, the clown slipped into the hall of the dolls' house, and went to the front door. In a moment he was outside and had shut the door! Good! Now the canary was quite safe and couldn't get out, because all the windows and doors were shut.

'Well, that's another good thing done!' said the clown, pleased. 'Amelia's caught – and the canary is safe!'

'Sh! Sh!' said the pink rabbit suddenly. 'Somebody is coming!'

'Gracious! And Amelia is in the cage!' said the little teddy bear.

They all scuttled to the toy-cupboard and lay down there, as still as could be. The door opened and in came Nanny. At first she didn't notice Amelia Jane in the cage and then she looked up and saw her. She stared and stared as if she couldn't really believe her eyes!

'Amelia Jane! In the canary's cage! And where is the canary?' cried the nanny in the greatest surprise. She hurried to the cage and looked inside.

'Why, the canary isn't here! Amelia Jane, what have you done with Goldie? Oh, you bad naughty doll, you are always in mischief of some sort!'

Nanny was very angry. She opened the cage-door and pulled Amelia Jane out rather roughly. Then she sat her down hard in the corner. Amelia Jane was very miserable.

Nanny looked everywhere for the canary, but of course she couldn't see Goldie. And

then the canary suddenly sang a little tune
from the dolls' house, and peeped out of a
window!

'Well, I never did!' cried Nanny, amazed. 'I
must be dreaming! Amelia in the canary's

cage – and the canary shut up in the dolls' house. Yes – I must be in bed and dreaming! But all the same I think I'll put Goldie back into his cage, dream or no dream!'

So she opened a window in the dolls' house, put in her hand and took hold of Goldie. She popped him back into his cage and shut the door. He was safe once more!

Then Nanny went out again to fetch the children from school. The toys peeped out from the cupboard at Amelia Jane. She was crying.

'How did you like being a canary in a cage?' asked the teddy bear.

'Sing us a little song!' said Tom.

'Spread your wings and fly!' said the pink rabbit.

And for once in a way Amelia didn't

answer back. She just turned her back on the toys and sulked. But they didn't mind that, you may be sure!

Poor Amelia Jane

Once it happened that some new people came to live next door to the house where Amelia Jane, the big naughty doll, lived. This was most exciting for the toys.

They did enjoy looking out of the window and seeing all the new furniture being taken out of the van.

'Oooh! What a big sideboard!' said the teddy bear. 'How will it go in at the front door?'

'Gracious! There must be lots of children there!' said Tom. 'I've seen three cots go in already.'

'One of them was a doll's cot, silly,' said

 157

Amelia Jane. 'I wonder if the new people will do anything to the garden. It's a dreadful mess.'

The new people did. They cut the grass and pulled up all the weeds. They pruned the trees and cut back the bushes. And then they dug a pond!

The toys were excited about that. '*We* haven't a pond in our garden,' said Amelia Jane. 'Now on moonlight nights we can take the toy boats and go and sail them there. And I can paddle.'

'That *will* be fun!' said the clockwork mouse. 'I must be careful not to drop my key in the pond, in case I can't find it again.'

The toys often sat on the window-sill watching the pond being dug. Then it was cemented all the way round, and crazy-paving was laid for an edging.

Then the pond was filled with water! It was great fun to watch. It trickled in and the pond was full by the evening.

And then the toys noticed something in the middle of the pond. It stuck out and seemed to be a kind of bowl with three little pipes.

'What's it for?' asked Amelia Jane.

'I think it is for a fountain,' said the bear, who had overheard somebody saying this. He didn't know what a fountain was – but he felt rather grand saying it, all the same.

'What's a fountain?' said Amelia Jane. 'Is it anything like a mountain?'

The toys didn't know. They had never seen a mountain or a fountain either. They stared at the thing in the middle of the pond.

'Oh, well, never mind,' said Amelia. 'It's

full moon tonight – what about taking the toy boats and going to sail them on the pond? That *would* be fun!'

So that night, when the moon was shining brightly, the toys all stole out of the nursery, and carried with them three little toy boats, a floating duck, and the toy ship. This was rather big, so the bear and Tom had to carry it together. With giggles and squeals they squeezed through the hedge into the next-door garden.

The pond looked lovely, shining in the moonlight. Amelia put one of the toy boats on the water and it floated beautifully. The pink rabbit put another boat into the pond and dragged it round and round by a bit of string. The clockwork mouse had a boat too. It was really fun. Then the bear launched the big ship, and it sailed right across the pond itself, bending sideways in the breeze.

The floating duck was overjoyed to have such a big piece of water to swim on, because usually she only had the bath. It was the clockwork mouse who had thought of bringing her, and she was really very grateful to him.

'Clockwork Mouse, would you like a sail on my back?' she called to him.

'Oh, I would,' said the mouse. 'All the other toys can paddle, but I can't, because I've only little wheels to run on instead of legs. Do take me for a ride on your back.'

'Clockwork Mouse, go to that funny thing in the middle of the pond and have a look at it!' said Amelia Jane suddenly. 'We can't wade there because the water gets too deep in the middle – but the duck can easily take you. Then you can climb up and run round the bowl there, and look into those three funny pipes.'

'He'd better not,' said the bear. 'We don't exactly know what that thing is for.'

'Oh, don't be so silly,' said Amelia, splashing the bear a little. She was paddling.

'What harm can he do?'

'Amelia Jane, if you splash me, I shall splash *you*!' said the bear crossly. Amelia Jane splashed him again.

Then the bear splashed Amelia so much that she ran out of the pond. 'You horrid bear! You've wetted my hair and you know it goes flat then. I don't like you!'

The clockwork mouse got on to the duck's back and the duck swam with him right to the middle of the pond. 'I think I'll just get off and look round this funny thing in the middle,' said the mouse. 'After all, I'm the only one that can really see what it is.'

So off he got and ran round the stone bowl. He looked into the three pipes too.

Now Amelia Jane was sulking a bit because the bear had driven her out of the pond by splashing so hard. She walked round to the other side of the pond – and she came across a pipe that led right down into the pond! And it had a tap on it. This was exciting!

Amelia Jane could never see a tap without turning it on, though she had been told again and again that it was a dangerous thing to do.

She tried to turn the tap – but it was very stiff. She used her right hand – then her left – and then she used both hands together!

The tap turned – and at the same moment the fountain began to play in the middle of the pond. *You* know what a fountain is, don't you? It's a big jet of water that gushes high into the air, turns over and falls back into the pond again! Well, that's just what happened when Amelia Jane turned on the tap!

Three jets of water gushed strongly out of the three pipes in the middle of the stone bowl in the pond, and sprang high into the air. They made a pretty arch before they fell back again, and all the toys stared in wonder at the fountain in the middle of the pond.

It shone in the moonlight. It made a pretty trickling noise – but what was that on top of it, jerking up and down on the water?

It was the poor little clockwork mouse! He had been looking at the pipes at exactly the same moment as Amelia had turned on the fountain – and the jets of water sprang high into the air and took him with them!

The mouse was astonished and frightened. He was jerked up and down at the top of the fountain, and he just couldn't do anything about it! The water held him there, and he

168

couldn't get down.

He began to squeak and squeal, and the toys stared in fright.

'The clockwork mouse is on top of the fountain! Look! He can't get out of it! It's bouncing the poor little thing up and down, up and down, and he must be getting terribly wet!'

Nobody knew that the fountain had been made because Amelia turned the tap on. But Amelia knew it, of course, and she tried her hardest to turn off the tap again. But she couldn't. Then she called to the toys to come and help but nobody was strong enough, not even Tom.

'Oh, you *are* tiresome, Amelia Jane!' said the pink rabbit, almost in tears, for he was very fond of the little mouse. 'You told the mouse to go and look at the fountain-thing – and then you go and turn on this tap and make the fountain come, and take the mouse up into the air with it! Now what are we going to do? The mouse will go on being bounced at the top of the fountain all night long!'

Amelia Jane was worried too. She didn't like to think of that. Whatever could be done? She tried to turn the tap off again – but it was far too stiff!

'I'd rescue him myself, but I can't walk,' said the toy duck. 'I'm no good out of the water.'

'Amelia Jane – you got the mouse into trouble, so you should be the one to get him out again,' said the bear, looking at the big doll.

'I know,' said Amelia. 'Well – there's only one way to rescue him, and that is for me to wade out into the very deep part, climb into the bowl, and try to reach the mouse with my hands. But the fountain will play over me if I do.'

'Serves you right,' said Tom.

Amelia Jane pulled her skirts above her knees and waded into the cold water. She took a few steps towards the middle of the pond. 'Ooooh! It's getting deep!' she said.

So it was – very deep! It was right above her waist by the time she got to the fountain. She pulled herself up into the stone bowl, which was now, of course, full of water. And then the fountain played all over poor Amelia Jane!

It wetted her yellow hair and her face.

It wetted her shoulders and ran down her neck! And when she reached up her arms to try to grab the clockwork mouse from the top of the fountain, the water ran down her sleeves! It went into her eyes and mouth, too, and she choked and spluttered.

But she got the mouse! She took hold of him and put him on her shoulder. Then she climbed down from the stone bowl into the pond again, and waded back to the bank. The clockwork mouse jumped down to the ground and shook himself free from the thousands of water drops all over him!

'Oh, that *was* a horrid adventure!' he squealed. The toys looked at him and hoped he wouldn't have a cold. If he had a cold and sneezed, his key flew out at each sneeze, and that was such a nuisance.

The toys all went back to the nursery, and Amelia Jane dripped like a fountain all the way! She had to undress herself, and sit in dry underwear in front of the gas-fire for the rest of the night. Her hair went all flat, and she really looked dreadful.

 173

'Well, it's a good punishment for you for interfering,' said Tom. 'But as you rescued the mouse so bravely, I really can't help feeling sorry for you. I'll put your hair in curl-papers if you like, and I'll help the bear to iron your clothes with the iron out of the dolls' house, when they are dry.'

'Thank you, Tom,' said Amelia, in a very small voice.

'Could you iron my tail too?' asked the mouse. But Tom said no, tails weren't meant to be ironed *or* put into curl-papers either.

When morning came, Amelia Jane was dry, her clothes were ironed, and her hair all bouncy again – and the clockwork mouse didn't get a cold, so things weren't as bad as they might have been!

Amelia Jane and the Drum

All the toys were as quiet as could be because
Nanny was in the room ironing. None of
them ever moved or spoke when anyone was
in the room.

'Bump-bump,' went Nanny's iron over the
ironing-board. 'Bump-bump.'

Tom and the baby doll were feeling proud because Nanny had washed their clothes that morning, and was now ironing them. How clean and pretty they would look in their freshly washed clothes!

Nanny finished ironing the little jackets, trousers, petticoats and dress.

She went to the nursery fireplace, and hung the little clothes on the brass rail round the guard to air.

Then she went out of the room to dress the children up nicely for their afternoon walk. Tom spoke up as soon as she had gone.

'Doesn't my jacket look lovely! Just look at it hanging there, so bright and clean!'

'And look at my lacy petticoats!' said the golden-haired doll, pleased. 'They will feel so nice and clean when I put them on again.'

Amelia Jane walked out of the toy-cupboard, and the toys followed her. 'What shall we play at?' asked Amelia. 'Let's play ring-a-ring-of-roses.'

'No, it's really too hot,' said the clockwork clown. 'Nanny has got the fire on today, and the sun is pouring in through the window. It's too hot to do anything but sit about and talk.'

'I *want* to play!' said Amelia Jane. So of course she made them all play with her! She was such a big doll and so strong that usually the toys just had to do what she told them. So there they were, tearing round and round in a big ring on the floor, singing ring-a-ring-of-roses in their small high voices.

'All fall down!' they cried. And down they all fell. The clockwork clown wouldn't get up again.

'No, really it's too hot,' he said. 'You look very hot yourself, Amelia Jane. You look red and ugly. Let's sit quietly and talk.'

'Dear me, if you're as hot as all that I'll open the window for you!' said Amelia Jane, who was feeling the heat herself by now.

'No, don't do that,' said the teddy bear. 'Nanny said she didn't want the window open because the wind was so strong.'

'I shall do as I like!' said Amelia Jane. And, as usual, she did! She went to the window-seat, climbed up on it, and got on to the window-sill. She undid the catch of the window and swung it wide open.

In came the wind at once. Whoo-oooo-ooooo-oooh!

'Oh, Amelia Jane! How naughty you are!' cried the clockwork clown. 'The wind has

blown over the vase of flowers on the table.
Look what a mess the water is making.'

'Nanny can clear it up,' said Amelia.

'And, oh, look, look, look!' suddenly
squealed the golden-haired doll. 'The wind is
blowing our clean clothes off the guard into
the fender. They'll go into the fire. Oh, oh,

what shall we do? Shut the window, Amelia Jane!'

But Amelia Jane couldn't! It had stuck and she wasn't strong enough to pull it back again. She stared at the little clothes blowing off the guard. The prettiest lace petticoat blew right into the fire and was burnt up!

'Oh!' screamed the golden-haired doll. 'There goes my best petticoat! Oh, you bad, mischievous doll!'

Amelia Jane didn't know what to do. She certainly was a bad doll, but all the same she didn't want to see the clothes burnt in the fire. The toys would never forgive her.

She called loudly: 'Nanny. Nanny! Come quickly!'

But Nanny didn't come. So Amelia called again: 'Nanny! Nanny!'

Still Nanny didn't come. She didn't hear. 'Oh, what shall I do?' cried Amelia Jane. The golden-haired doll sobbed. Tom glared at Amelia.

Then Amelia had a bright idea. She rushed to the toy-cupboard. She reached right to the back of it, and took out the toy drum. She found two sticks. And then she went to the nursery door and banged hard on that little drum.

'Rum-ti-tum-ti-tum! Rum-ti-tum-ti-tum! Rr-rr-rr-rr-rr-rr-rr!Rum-ti-tum-ti-tum!'

You should have heard the noise! My goodness, it was deafening! Nanny heard it. The children heard it. They listened in great astonishment.

'That's my drum!' cried the little boy. 'Who is playing it? Who can it be?'

The two children and Nanny ran to see. As soon as Amelia heard them coming she flung the drum down on the floor and raced back to the toy-cupboard with the toys. They sat down there and kept as still as could be. Nanny and the children could see nothing at all when they came into the nursery – except the little drum thrown down on the floor with its two sticks lying beside it.

'How funny!' said Nanny. 'Who played the

drum? And why?'

'Nanny! Nanny! The dolls' clothes are blowing off the guard into the fire!' cried the little girl. 'Oh look!'

Nanny rushed to save them. Alas, they were all dirty again now, and would have to be washed and ironed once more. And one petticoat was quite gone.

'Who opened that window?' said Nanny crossly. 'I left it shut. I knew the clothes would blow into the fire if the wind came into the room. And look – it's blown over the flowers on the table, too. What a mess! I wish I knew who had opened that window. They deserve a good telling off.'

Amelia Jane went red. The toys looked at her and nodded their heads. Yes – she did deserve a good telling off!

When Nanny and the children had gone out for their walk the baby doll spoke angrily to naughty Amelia Jane.

'I shan't be able to wear my clothes today. All because of you, Amelia Jane. Nanny is right – you do deserve a good scolding.'

'And what about my clothes, too?' said Tom gloomily. 'My trousers were scorched by the flames. They will never look so nice again, just round the waist.'

Amelia Jane was very red. She took off her new hair-ribbon and held it out to Tom. 'You can have this to tie round your waist for a sash,' she said. 'Then it will hide the bit that is scorched. And Golden-haired Doll – I will get six of my little handkerchiefs and sew them together to make a small petticoat for you.'

'Well, it is nice of you to try and make up for what we have lost,' said the golden-haired doll. 'Perhaps we won't be cross with you after all.'

'Well, I *did* think of the drum and beat it to get somebody here to rescue your clothes,' said Amelia Jane. 'Didn't I?'

'Yes, that was clever of you,' said Tom. 'All right we'll forgive you this once, Amelia. But DON'T BE SILLY AGAIN!'

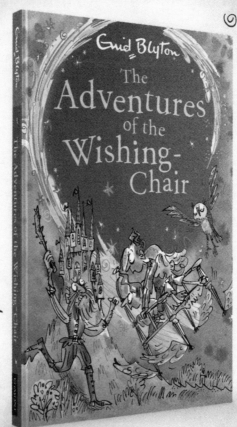